The ship goes "Blip."

One ship goes "OOPS!"

For my father (who loves a good robot)

 All our books are Smyth Sewn (the highest library-quality binding available) and printed with soy-based inks on acid-free, woodfree paper harvested from responsible sources. Printed in China by C&C Offset Printing Co., Ltd. Distributed to the trade by Consortium Book Sales; orders (800) 283-3572; orderentry@perseusbooks.com; www.cbsd.com. Library of Congress Cataloging-in-Publication Data available at http://lccn.loc.gov/2016003369 See our free cartoon makers, lesson plans and more at www.TOON-BOOKS.com.

ISBN: 978-1-935179-98-6 (hardcover)

16 17 18 19 20 21 C&C 10 9 8 7 6 5 4 3 2 1

A TOON BOOK BY

Barnaby Richards

BLIP!

BLIP?
BANG!

BANG!
BANG!

BANG!
BANG!
BLIP,
BLIP!

?
SHHHHHHHHH

BLIP?

BLIP?
I'm *not* a BLIP!

?
I am a-

RUN!

ROAAR
BLEEEEEP!

OOF!

BLIP?

Blip! Blip! Blip! Blip! Blip! Blip! Blip! Blip!

Blip! Blip! Blip! Blip! Blip! Blip! Blip! Blip! Blip! Blip! Blip! Blip! Blip! Blip!

Blip!
Blip! Blip!
BLIP?

BLIP!

BOO!

BOO!

SPLASH!

BLIP?

BOO?

SPLASH!

SNAP!
BLEEEEP!

BLIP!
OOF!
?

BLIP!

BOO!
AHHHH!

BLIP!
That's no way to say "hello"!

BLIP!
Goodbye!

BLIP!
SNIFF!

Blip! Blip! Blip! Blip! Blip!

SNIFF!
SNIFF!
SNIFF!

N
S

ANG!
BANG!
NG!
BANG!
?

BANG!
BANG!
BANG!

BANG!
BANG!
BANG!
BANG!
BANG!
BANG

!
BANG!
BANG!

BLIP?
BLEEP!

BLEEP!
BLIP-BLIP!

BLIP!

ABOUT THE AUTHOR

Barnaby Richards lives in London, where he shares a studio with his wife Alice and their cat Mosca. He has been doodling pictures of his little robot in the margins of notebooks and the corners of pictures for many years.

Barnaby was inspired to write *Blip!* when he felt it was time his robot found a friend.

See you!
Goodbye!
Blip blip blip blip blip BLIP!
BOO?
BLIP-BLIP BLEEP BLIP BLIP BLIBLIP BLIP BLIP BLEEEEP BLIP?
BLIP!

"Blip!" goes the ship, and off they go.

TIPS FOR PARENTS AND TEACHERS:

HOW TO READ COMICS WITH KIDS

Kids love comics! They are naturally drawn to the details in the pictures, which make them want to read the words. Comics beg for repeated readings and let both emerging and reluctant readers enjoy complex stories with a rich vocabulary. But since comics have their own grammar, here are a few tips for reading them with kids:

GUIDE YOUNG READERS: Use your finger to show your place in the text, but keep it at the bottom of the speaking character so it doesn't hide the very important facial expressions.

HAM IT UP! Think of the comic book story as a play and don't hesitate to read with expression and intonation. Assign parts or get kids to supply the sound effects, a great way to reinforce phonics skills.

LET THEM GUESS. Comics provide lots of context for the words, so emerging readers can make informed guesses. Like jigsaw puzzles, comics ask readers to make connections, so check a young audience's understanding by asking "What's this character thinking?" (but don't be surprised if a kid finds some of the comics' subtle details faster than you).

TALK ABOUT THE PICTURES. Point out how the artist paces the story with pauses (silent panels) or speeded-up action (a burst of short panels). Discuss how the size and shape of the panels carry meaning.

ABOVE ALL, ENJOY! There is of course never one right way to read, so go for the shared pleasure. Once children make the story happen in their imagination, they have discovered the thrill of reading, and you won't be able to stop them. At that point, just go get them more books, and more comics.